Keith Althaus

NEW & SELECTED POEMS

Grid Books, 2024

Grid Books
Boston, MA
www.grid-books.org

Cover: Painting by Susan Baker, "Near York" (detail), 1999, acrylic on canvas, 16 x 20 in., collection of the artist.

Grateful acknowledgment is made to the editors of the following journals for publishing poems included in this collection: *Cape Cod Poetry Review, The Cape Cod Times, The Cincinnati Review, Harvard Review,* and *Ploughshares.*

Printed in the United States of America. Book design by Michael Alpert.

ISBN: 978-1-946830-20-3

For Claire—

and Zella and Vincent—

and in memory

of my brother Paul

Table of Contents

Selected Poems

from Rival Heavens (1993)

from Ladder of Hours (2005)

from Cold Storage (2016)

Have you learned to love spring yet,
even a little? I have,
just enough to experience
the havoc and recklessness
without tears,
like the removal of bandages
in front of a mirror.

New Poems

At the End of Your Street

At the end of your street
the sky softens the hard outline
of buildings and things
that do nothing but watch
as the light does all the work,
filling in between branches and leaves,
painting the corners black, the way
you go to sleep, at the edges, first
not thinking, then letting yourself
be changed, this much anyway,
questioning nothing though many things
have gone wrong, and what you did,
errors you made, knew at the time,
remain like stones; and how many years
of incessant wind and rain
will it take to wear them down
till you see clearly again the end of the street,
whether it is Naples or Kiev, Brooklyn or Rome?

The Letters

When I see gold letters in the air
above a classroom or banquet hall
I don't care if they spell *Welcome Home*
or *Happy Anniversary* they remind me
of the Annunciation and the barely
visible scroll that unfurls between
the Angel Gabriel and the Virgin Mary
when she's told whose child she'll bear.
And whether it's transmitted aurally
or telepathically it still gives me pleasure
to see them turn and sway, gleaming
in the air, trembling when someone
bumps the wire on which they're strung.
But it means no more than the three
telephone poles on a hillside, or workers
carrying a rug down a flight of stairs.

Old beliefs, demoted to mere suggestions,
superstitions, yet every letter remains
a gate, heavy, ornate, that can still be used
to open a chapter, or start a sentence
which may become a meme, a way of saying
that goes on, held aloft by a tiny plane
sputtering above the crowded beach.

Poem

Better than a mirror,
this black window at midnight,
more drama, less detail;
also next to nothing
of the room where you hid
since you crossed out *poet*
and wrote in *theologian* instead.

Call it what you will,
it is the same spiral staircase
you've been climbing all your life:
from jungle gyms and monkey bars,
to man-made rock walls
and marked trails where
beauty comes to a halt,
because at these heights
it cannot breathe,
its lights reduced to glints
like far-off stars.

A life can be distilled
into a few important tears
sprinkled over earth
like holy water:
rhinestones melting on the lawn,
a glimpse of new-born skin
as bark rolls off a branch
spinning in a culvert,
the needle of a compass.

Kindergarten Statistics

The prisoners of tomorrow
are sitting at their desks
opening cartons of milk
like little houses,
getting crumbs
over everything.

You pick: this one
is tall for his age,
but awkward,
shrinks from contact,
yet has the sweetest smile.
That one is always moving,
either from the joy
of being alive, or dread
of something catching him.
And she, she rambles
in and out of song,
a bubbly mosaic
made of sound.

The experts agree
a certain percent
will end up dead
or incarcerated by thirty.
Just as others will be
rich or bald.

If our fates hovered
over us like the pennants
tour guides raise
to call their flocks,
would we even notice,
bent to focus
on our struggle
to break these chains
which, should we succeed,
would only, by necessity
and the laws of mathematics,
fall on someone else?

Scene on 10th Street

The young clambering
for the mausoleum,
dark museum
of their thought,
desire to be
on a mountaintop
where the winds
drive away all doubt.

Three-wide, coming
down the sidewalk
toward us, one
gesticulating wildly,
but precise, like
a conductor, the others
juggling, controlling
laughter like a bubble
made improbably
of words.

Events under a sky
no longer fabulous,
but tamed, falconless.
The blood on their jeans
alizarin crimson.

Still Life with Beads

Motionless,
the light and air
in the spare bedrooms
of grown children,
brightened by the removal
of a big tree whose arms fell over
shoulders bent in thought,
planning everything,
even antiquating with a flame
the deckled edge of a treasure map,
whose X, to this day, goes unclaimed.

Like large objects placed
in aquariums, the sturdy furniture
they call simply brown today:
desk and chair and heavy dresser,
with a lamp and a jar of foreign coins
to pay, no doubt, the ferryman,
place on eyes no longer moving,
the way you'd drop a clod
on the back of a struggling beetle
in the sand, to be unkind,
show you're one of us.

A cracked tankard
holds a bouquet
of verticals: pencils, rulers,
the drooping peacock feather,
a slide rule in its crumbling

leather case, and poised
along the rim as if
about to escape,
a short length of beads
partly obscuring the tavern scene,
worn, dull, ordinary,
from a marketplace in India,
cold and raining,
where they joined for life.

If the way is impassable,
why do pilgrimages keep springing up,
starting with a word, or image,
after a night of drinking,
when Orion's Belt lay on the blacktop
sputtering like a fuse
unable to ignite
the piles of weeds pulled up
along the walk.

Poem

Put your shoes and socks
in the cubby. We'll go
barefoot the rest of the way.

Over bricks like these
which tapped together
clink and show they are
both light and heavy.

Who knows if the sun
will ever return
to the lasso-trimmed shade
above the plastic cactus
and the palomino,
or if green like this
even exists in heaven?
Why are there no originals here?
only reproductions,
weak, washed-out colors,
to remind us
of purer, sharper hues,
the way our shapes
are redrawn more coarsely every day
with each successive generation,
moving us further from the source?
Degradation by duplication:
The Law of Xerox.

Think of the carved capitals
at Autun and Moissac:
        solid blocks of art,
out of nothing, like nothing,
not even the cubes of soft wood
they hand you
to start whittling—
        mine's around here someplace—
with the implicit instruction
they look like something,
        undermining
the prescience of rainy afternoons
        when we are sometimes
moved into the future
        and for a moment
lose the terms of our imprisonment:
the moat reduced to puddles
under the swings and slide.

Late Bus, Provincetown

What did we want from our lives?

Someone has taken
the question mark
and hammered it
back into a stick,
just as they have
straightened the roads
whose very turning
was their beauty.

Recently on the side
of a building
on the town wharf
a local photographer has installed
four large black-and-white panels,
close-ups of old Portuguese women,
fishermen's wives.
They look out
all day, all night,
on the harbor, listen
to the Town Hall bell
after the last bus has arrived
and departed and the last couple
has passed under or around
the lampposts' cones of light.

The faces are meant
to stir within us

both a sense of the tragic
frailty and the harshness
of life, made bearable
only by the beauty
of courage and sacrifice.
Unlike the granite monument
on top of the hill which feels
the wind and rain and snow
intermittently, these faces
are exposed every day
to the spray of the surf
and are soaked
by the tides below.
Already they've been
taken down twice
for repair and restoration.
Yet their eyes never blink
or close like a doll's
laid on its back.
They do not look, but stare
at everything: the breakwater,
floats, gulls, the fleet
coming in, trailing clouds
of bird life, raucous,
joyful as a sudden
whirlwind of litter
on a corner in the city.

Ruins

For miles
nothing else
around,
standing out
like the gate
in a wall
that's torn down,
the city
it protected
no more
than slight mounds
and depressions
where its
towers, keep,
and granaries were.

Columns and trees,
clumped together
like the setting
of a pastoral,
or one of the giant
letters that begins
a book,
tall enough
to walk through,
lead a cow
between
ivied arches,
where you could

lean against
the curving wall
or sit upon
a toppled stone
expressing languor
in a song
while birds
in pairs
nesting in the crannies
hidden by a curtain
of green
panic over nothing.

Provincetown White Line Print

The fog rolls in
cold and thick
between the buildings,
obliterating details
of modern life:
sliders, antennas,
telephone poles,
leaving just
the white outline
of a fishing village,
and you get a sense
of what it was like
years ago, until
your reverie is broken
by an approaching car
or the fog's sudden
lifting to reveal
flowers and trees
on a lawn that came
from China as ballast
on a clipper ship.

On the Representation of Tropical Birds in Pennsylvania German Fraktur

Those exotics, seemingly the products of the mind's extension,
reaching out from darkness toward a light not native to this place
of iron, wood, and stone, were real, and not invented:
Carolina Parakeets, now extinct, that dwelled among these hills,
farmlands-to-be; their yellow, green wings flew through primeval
forests of oak and fir, a blur, as if they'd veered off course,
been blown north, an island migration gone astray centuries before,
and brought the unimaginable jungle here, a thought unlike the rest
but like a day in summer that will stand for paradise.

Art History

Forget all the shuffling
and sorting of slides
and cards: piles of rare
moments and rich detail:
masterpieces
with corners bent.
The trick is to follow the path
that leads here, wherever *here* is.
It may be a place of stone tears,
silent machinery, and tools
under layers of dust
from finished monuments.
Or it might be
a pencil-stroke forest
you can't get out of
as long as the artist's hand
is turned around, facing you,
seeking a likeness.
It's as simple as this:
Beauty is backlit by death.

On the Removal of the Statue of Frank Rizzo from Center City, Philadelphia

Like a scene out of the post-war Italian cinema:
sailing over the city at midnight,
trussed up and lifted leaning forward
like a figurehead, minus the boat:
the larger-than-life statue of Frank Rizzo,
Mayor of Philadelphia, cop
who yelled "Vote white!"
now ordered removed by the city council
and the mayor's office,
from its base in City Hall Plaza
to an undisclosed location,
temporarily in limbo, a place
even the Pope is not sure exists.

Bric-a-Brac

"The trouble with you, Robert,
is that you write about—subjects."
"The trouble with you, Wallace,
is that you write about—bric-a-brac."
– Meeting between Frost and Stevens

After the storm,
when the green clouds leave,
retreating over mounds
of shard-filled rubble,
the desperate climb those hills
looking for . . . what?
Irreplaceable nothings:
a yearbook with its falling-out bits
of ribbon and lace;
bent, and now warped Polaroids,
with red eyes,
and a wedding album
they must find a place
to spread out and dry.
And medals and letters.
Any other time, big-ticket items:
a good position, solid investments,
would give comfort,
but this morning, to the still
shaken, moaning scavengers
on the heaps of their lives,
the discovery of a purple glass
peacock, miraculously unbroken,

speaks to them and weighs more
than the missing bathroom scale
could ever say.

Forms

He says he works in forms too.
By which he means those heavy boards,
thick sheets of plywood they set up
exactly in the ground and then pour
concrete into. You've seen them
in place waiting, or bundled up
on trucks ready to go. "It's not the same"
I don't say, not sure if it is or isn't.
Neither of us travels light. He has
scars and places that will always ache.
I have tics, recurrent thoughts I can't
escape, they find me, almost free
at midnight, the armor put away, but then. . . .
So I say yes, we both work in forms.

The Widow

Her tour bus stops at the Ephrata Cloister, an 18th century religious community in Lancaster County, Pennsylvania.

All day through intermittent rain,
so many things to say, share:
silly signs, a view, the changes
a few years have made,
but running through it now,
absence, like a hole,
as if everything were hollow,
just for show, for the survivor,
revisiting places seen together:
a landscape shining with rain,
the *Dutch Country* absorbing
another wave of change,
the first already aging
and in the way. Skittering
drops streak and blur
the window and drying
leave it not clearer but
duller, the way tears
meant to lighten the soul
only seem to make it darker.

The ride home quiet,
subdued, the landscape at dusk
revealing glimpses of what
it withheld all day: an unfinished
bank abutting a fieldstone farmhouse,

the same stone in piles raked
from the new lawn;
and seen between houses,
narrow backyards that end
abruptly in a cornfield,
a freshly painted outhouse.
After the rain, purple and black
clothes hanging on the line.
Sunlight on a fading hex sign.
On the barn hill grass filling in
the tire tracks, a gate held open
by vines, inside hedges
lost fences sag under mounds
of honeysuckle, and farm ponds
swarm with algae
like the shadows of clouds.

The accumulation of details,
fragments, partial views,
forms a subliminal landscape
the way a child's face
resembles the parents'.

Tonight she will recall,
like some of the others,
the block of wood
that was their pillow,
not the austere buildings
and tidy grounds they

wandered, or the rote explanations
of the robed guide,
but the pillow,
the wood darkened, worn,
where they laid their heads,
that and the absence
which followed her,
turning from the aisle
to the window, where
sudden thoughts, unique
as snowflakes, melted
into drops without distinction.

Portrait of Ellery, Age Three, On the Studio Floor

Grotesques wait
outside your playpen.

Handmade giants peer
through plastic mesh.

Your mother set you here
to watch you grow

among the products
of her intellect,

which grew inside of her
just like you,

until she let them go
and each became

"the death-mask
of its conception."

So commenced
their afterlife as art.

You, our counterweight,
crawl and climb

on all fours
in all directions,

as a compass spins
between magnets,

heart and mind,
or just two hearts.

Poem

All the houses you lived in,
rooms where you studied,
are one house now, one room
where you study still, love
and its missing pages.

Sue at Seashore Point

Hardly the same
as the Women's House of Detention,
in Greenwich Village, where lovers,
mothers, sisters, children
stood in the street
and yelled up
through the noisy dirty air
to the upper floors
where their loved ones were being held.

We didn't have to raise our voices,
or only slightly, to get the words
to bend back up to your ear,
after we'd leaned down and spoken
into the three-inch opening
between the sash and sill,
still screened in
though it was October.

What we said
was all encouraging,
real or fake,
and from your side:
defiance and complaint,
railing at attendants, nurses,
supplies, the inoperable controls
to the bed, black TV,
and dead phone.

You vowed to resist and did,
getting out in a record two days,
but leaving behind a brooch,
and a library book we had to pay for,
and the other families
huddled under eaves, standing
in flower beds, frozen
in the iconic but antiquated
pose of listening,
as if to a World Series
or the reassuring words
of a President abjuring fear.

Poem

I have moved against all magic
in borrowed, rented rooms,
where the water of the moon
flows through the spigot,
and the wallpaper takes down
its book of yellowed days.
On the roof bullets of the rain
beat out a furious message
and in the field a tree,
a well, a gate stand in unison
like animals too dumb or proud
to come in or have no home.

Santa Croce

The great rose window
like an exhaust fan
to take away the smoke
of guttered candles, and stale prayers,
while new hope enters
under the tympanum's flying wedge
where a crowd huddles triumphantly
waiting for the kingdom to come
from a marble cloud.

The air inside is blessed,
re-blessed: words heard a million times
so even stone ears can understand.
You've come to say goodbye
to the sea-green Annunciation:
the Virgin pulling back, reacting
to the news like the chill of the tide.

Poem

Every poem is a grave,
and what's buried there
even the digger,
the one with the pen
doesn't know.
Every word,
every shovelful,
is a mask
of tragedy or comedy,
that leaves the world
with a hole.
We trade
our box of air
for a box of dirt,
that weighs the same—
nothing—zero—
the empty egg that gives birth
to numbers that don't add up
to infinity, but always fall
one short.

Homage

These days when I see
AI printed boldly
in the papers,
instead of picturing
the uncertain future
they're trying to portray,
I see the mournful face
of a woman who gave us,
year after year, poems
like battered flophouse doors
and walls about to tear.

Afterlife

For a while
after someone dies
you can still see them:
out of a corner
of your eye,
even straight on,
at a window
as it glides
through the station.

Those people
are always there,
but then
we stop seeing them,
or we see them but
they don't look like
whoever died anymore.
At least not enough
to take your breath.

Perhaps we're all stand-ins,
lookalikes, for someone else,
maybe living in the next town,
who takes the bus each day.
Why not? You've been
mistaken many times
in the street, looked at oddly
at a concert by someone
doubly surprised

you're not their friend
and their friend is dead.

That period is short-lived
the Tibetans say,
forty days,
it's natural, and always fades.
Then come dreams,
no limit there—
everyone lives forever,
or at least
as long as breath
advances the plot.

There you recognize
them by their names,
until they give those up.
Then you hear:
"It was her,
but it didn't look like her."
Or, "He called himself Stefan.
but I know it was Ted."

Now they are just extras,
standing around,
waiting for their stones.

Murmuration

The murmuration of starlings
in the air above the bus station in Rome
brought huge crowds every night
at dusk to see them swirl and dive
and tumble and erase themselves
like an Etch-a-Sketch.

They are not here
for our entertainment,
or even study—bordering
on the spiritual, mystical
side of things—but to obey
the primordial command
of magnets under the road,
on the rooftops of garages,
in the core of great machines,
cold and dark, called immobile
but in reality travelling
with us at enormous speed.

We are waiting for
our "Damascus Road/My name is Tania" moment,
as a shadow climbs
the white-washed stairs.

Poem

The beauty of the world
increases as we get older.
Our friends get thinner
or non-existent, ghosts
take up a lot of room.

On the other hand
as the clock gets louder
we cannot hear it,
just as people living
in stinking mill towns
say after awhile
you don't notice.

We are holding hands
with x, if x equals the time
we have, unknowable of course,
and changing with each breath.

The air is richer
in these little rooms
like overcrowded elevators
going down. Yet so much
oxygen toward the end,
like living on sweets.

From the Mezzanine

Brigham & Women's Hospital, Boston

1.

Placed here
like Katz's people
on the wall
but freer
to move
and not just stare.
We are more than ink
skin-deep
or cool flat colors
interacting;
we are storms,
real events, feelings,
even including
our narcissistic desire
to die on stage.

Prayers,
wishes, echo silently
off out-of-reach hospital walls,
cliffs whose faces reflect precisely
our diminished selves.
At the railing
we confront the edge's
antique dare.

2.

In the atrium today
I saw for the first time
the *mobile* of autumn leaves,
hundreds suspended along
invisible wires between floors,
evenly spaced, plain brown
and yellow, hardly any enflamed
like out-of-doors,
and perfectly still
because the door
downstairs is closed
for Covid-19.

Is it one enormous
Christmas ornament
they bring out, put up,
and take down each year?
If I'm lucky will I see it again
next year, possibly
in motion, the door below
opening and closing,
the virus disappeared?
And our questions and the answers
they were chasing,
where will they be then?

Poem for My Brother

The god to whom
I would have prayed for you tonight
is gone where mirages go
when you stop the car
and get out.
He went away, left
long before this,
though I couldn't say.
How could they
be wrong, not see;
how could they see
what wasn't there?
A stinging thought.

None of it matters
tonight as you are
locked in battle:
alien bodies swim
in your blood and those
you've put your faith in
can't get them out.

The hours, which were
never your friends,
have ganged up on you.
Time swells and carries
you along a stream
of familiar debris,
past buildings you walked by

as a boy. There must be
something sticking out
that you can grab a hold of:

how about that old antenna
that brought in Havana
and Moscow, or the pole
you used to push off
from the bank your raft
of scavenged boards and canvas,
while the cheers and shouts
from the shore instead of dying down
got louder, and the laughter
was edged with fear
as one corner of the float
went under and you
began to disappear?

Poem

You will never finish your life
the way you intended.
The bed you will never get up from
is not the one you wanted,
by a lake or river's edge
where the light touches
each bird awake
except the one
that kept watch all night.

Poem

We read Nabokov backwards
like grad students
in newspaper hats
that could easily turn into boats
if we started sinking.
And the leaves were young on the trees.
And the leaves were young on the trees.

Years Later

he told me
what happened
after I'd left—
the suicide attempt.
And it all suddenly
fit together. Even
among so many wasted days
that afternoon always
stood apart for its,
as we would have said then—
strange vibes.

Odd to think of it now,
back in the brain
making the adjustment,
changing the story,
replacing one fact, no longer,
with another.

Tonight I am like
an old painter
reworking an early canvas,
changing the light source,
adjusting the shadows.

Chamber Music, Saturday Morning, The Truro Public Library

So few souls . . .
that's what they called the serfs
in 19th century Russia, in all those books
you saved but that in the end couldn't save you back.
I would have thought a better turnout,
more like the Second Coming
but without the judgment, just the music,
"the wind that sweeps the streets of heaven."
Among believers, and I'm not one,
there's disagreement over who and what gets in.
And do they sleep? and dream, or ever weep?
Do lawns up there need mowing too?
Does anything even grow? This might
be the best of it, and it leans down
this morning in this half-filled room.

Leaving the Party

I'm stuck!
having allowed myself
to drift into this corner,
a lazy backwater, away
from the center stage
where the double-edged swords,
career and gossip,
hack away at each other
and accidentally destroy
the golden haze
of perfume and smoke.

Up against a bookcase
reading sideways
names we knew
before they climbed
those spines and became
"voices of a generation."
I almost expect to see tiny archers
leap from the crenelated tops
of books and pierce us
with reminders of our mission.

I would like to hear a poem now,
feel its weighted line
in my palm
like a sudden order:
Stay where you are!

The paper trembling
like an origami bird unfolding,
becoming again
a wrapper of gum.

My drink done
years ago.
Last friend
moved away,
lost, or fallen
backwards like one
stopping on the sidewalk
to tie a shoe,
becomes an eddy
in the dream.

Let the questions begin,
already pared
to a great few:
The Problem of Evil;
Original Sin;
and if no other,
The Place of Pain
in the Universe.

Are we talking now,
or is this just
an echo chamber?

If devils walked on Earth,
not just hurt children
but pure evil
instead of victims
of victims,
would it be easier?
Could we then at last
untie the simplest, hardest
tear-soaked knot?

I should go.
The party is reaching
its zenith, loud,
high-pitched drone,
and I haven't found out
yet why I came.
I should go,
through a sea
of bobbing faces,
all eyes on the door.
I must make
my goodbyes.

Osawatomie

When my mother said,
sometime in her eighties,
that she'd never known
anyone as old as she was,
I thought instantly
of the white-bearded men
who paraded as the last veterans
of the Civil War in newsreels
that flickered and crackled
like campfires.

She was from Missouri,
land of Quantrill's Raiders,
segregated schools,
and not too far from Osawatomie.
She was going back
in her mind, over her
parent's friends, elders
and beyond, the oldest
of the old, yet finding
no one older than herself:
still alive, living on her own,
and driving! How many
years ago was that?

We lived in York,
not far from Gettysburg,
where low walls of the same stone
surrounded the fields, but where

they manufactured chain and cable
instead of shoes, which soldiers need:
maybe it was only that
the creeks were too deep
to ford, or one town lacked
higher ground—accidents of Fate,
that multi-purpose word
in which unexplained events
are bundled together like sheaves
standing vigil in a field at night
for the dead and injured
and the living who cannot sleep.

Poem

Those who come back from the dead
often say there is an extra hour
in the day that goes unnoticed
by most of us who've never been
anywhere, that falls between
the brightness of the afternoon
and when the dark takes back
the last fringe of light, or when
everybody suddenly leaves a room,
or all but one, who doesn't speak
but stares out the window
at nothingness the way children do,
shifting their weight from heel to heel.
It is where they go while we are
talking, taking notes, making plans
on paper already on fire.

Snow Globe

The whole town, streets
and intersections buried
now with treetops, steeples,
lampposts sticking up,
boxy schools and factories,
fabricating plants
and showrooms, corner
taverns and row houses
covered like furniture
in country homes
closed for the season,
under cloths that sweep
the floor like wind-carved drifts.

The Square

In the York, PA, where I grew up
it was a tradition for art students
from the public schools to decorate
the windows of the downtown
stores with Halloween-themed pictures.

Over the crow's black shoulder
you pick out a world:
thelakeslashskatingrink
where scarves are drawn
into long sentences that leave
the reader breathless, pale,
the dog cut off mid-bark.

The alternation of work and play,
duty and pleasure,
and their intersection:
the making of toys,
the baking of dessert.

Is it a joke, or a curse
that at the end of the telescope
there's a cameo of you
upside down, a brooch
to wear at midnight,
carry all day in a purse,
like a newly minted coin,
both heads and tails.

– *After Brueghel*

1.

Down from your
perch above the town
on the cast-iron arm of a lamppost
like a gargoyle or bird of prey,

watching closely the events of the day unfold:
an unexpected procession of pedestrians
from all corners of the city,
dots of India ink or lead filings
dragged across a map.

On closer examination
they're just children,
not going to school,
taking another route
and wearing play clothes,
though it's a weekday morning:
drab hats and coats, at most a hunter's bold plaid
(this is years before dayglo and neon colors),
making their way through intersections,
across parks and neighborhoods,
so many moving parts, heading for
a pre-arranged destination
in the Square where a panel truck
is already dispensing to-go containers
of tempera paint, brushes, rags:
the three primaries plus black and white,
and a tall water in sturdy cardboard cups,

along with instructions on behavior
and cleanup, a map of the windows
to be painted, plus your "original," scored
with a pencil grid and ready for
enlargement and transfer to plate glass.

Teachers, assistants, parent-volunteers
helping to measure, tape, set up
step ladders and drop cloths, hastening
the disappearance of this year's
back-to-school and Fall collections,
shunted into gloomy ante-rooms
before the frenzy of Xmas.

2.

The stragglers weave their way
through tree-lined neighborhoods
like members of a disbanded horde,
assured by the sight of a piece
of their history surviving intact:
a familiar name, perhaps
hyphenated by now but not entirely lost.
These had the hardest time this morning
separating from their dreams. They are
the same ones who, if any, will notice
and connect disparate elements blocks apart
in new configurations rather than fit
them all in the same old slots
to the same songs of self-congratulation.

3.

The grownup trees
no longer fear the knife,
the blade that could hack
and slice, roll back
the old skin revealing
white beneath
in an act of love
or self-aggrandizement
aimed at eyes yet unborn,
an imagined permanence,
though considerably hampered
by the choice of trees,
their barely legible,
initialed and pierced lop-sided
hearts half-submerged
in a sea of troughed
and gullied bark.

4.

Window by window
along the sidewalk,
pages in a giant book.
Varied methods, styles
techniques . . .
from slavish imitation,
the swept-up girlish faces
with Egyptian eyes,
to the strong black line of comix,

confining washed-out pixels
like souls evaporating in prison.
Does this line descend
from the stained glass
whose lead
grips tightly the solid light
of jewels, loaded with color
and molded to the shoulders
of prophets and saints
about to be martyred,
pushed to the flames.

5.
A bloated pumpkin
fills the window
so completely
there's no room left
for anything but a pair
of green slippers in the corner
at the bottom and a blue sash
across the top. In the window
next door a bat's gray felt wing
is stretched like a banner
between kite sticks while blood
dribbles buttons down a vest.

A memory of the future,
the howling wind tunnel
of the sixties.

Historic youth in turbulent streets.
Bread and Puppet's unwieldy
two-story giant teeters,
then proceeds,
to the solemn beat
of thunder's drum.

6.
Two things are missing
from this exhibit:
the one will surface later,
like a body in a river,
complete with guilty ropes
and weights. The empty
dungeon scene, done
in a clumsy hand, is
but a premonition. Who
will correct the spelling
of the writing on the wall?

The other is articulate
beyond words:
abstraction, non-objective:
art dismissed instinctively,
before there was a *Riverwalk,*
or *Spring-Art-A-Thon,* let alone
an *Armory Show.* Still,
shunned, unframed and leaning
against the chain-link fence

or hung from a clothesline
it is inexpressively concrete,
realer than real!
approaching the ultimate reality:
the placebo.

Once considered one
of the century's
intellectual scams like
the "talking cure,"
ridiculed until it armed
itself with working drugs.
These orphans of a failed
persuasion are accepted now
only because of their corporate
sponsorship and amazing auction records.
A begrudging disbelief shines
through dismissive smiles.

There will never be
another moment,
shared or reflected, like this:
an idyll of such sweetness,
loyalty and awe,
as in that photograph
of Red Army troops,
in their civil war,
sprawled on a hillside,
smoking, a lull

in the action, in a grove
of unfamiliar trees,
bivouacked beneath
the black square
of Malevich.

7.
By noon it's more than
half over and there's no
school after, an early day.
Freedom! Though for most,
alone, without friends,
because only one or two
were chosen from each class,
each school, city-wide.

Going home,
leaving civilization,
unlearning, reverting
to the wild and tame at once,
a growing strangeness
to the familiar, like walking
backwards past that non-descript
temple of commerce
the Farmers' Market, tucked away
like Borromini's secret church
in downtown Rome.

Built by master shipwrights
from up and down the Chesapeake.
Awe-inducing height
is part of the cathedral experience:
vertigo itself may be an element
of belief, but here it's hard
to know the purpose of those
great gulps of light and air between
the buttresses and golden vaults
in the sight of impractical windows,
sky-high and unreachable.

On the floor below
a network of aisles and vendors' stalls
glows beneath the lattice of wires
and chain holding up long fluorescent
bulbs above bright tomatoes, peppers,
beans and corn. Today one stall
is devoted to cards and prints
of local historic scenes: the replica
courthouse, the Plough Tavern and Gates House,
the Cookes House, made from a vein
of blue limestone that runs from
the Susquehanna west for fifty miles,
a strip of moonlight, the lantern path
of the Continental Congress fleeing
the Redcoats. It was Tom Paine
who wrote *The Crisis* there by candlelight.

8.

In the late October sun
the last mark is made on a checklist
and the truck drives off
loaded with cardboard barrels
(this was before
the plastic garbage bag)
and the Square returns to normal:
shoppers, office workers, some
slow to look, note a change,
the advance of orange and brown,
like fields rising out of sidewalks,
with multiple moons and scythes
scattered on the horizon.
From above the Square looks like
a pocket watch with its back taken off
and revealing circular openings like wells
or manholes, all doing something different.
In one an old wooden kiosk,
left over from the days when buses
and trolleys ran here, the quaintness
wearing off; in another, a new low
brick planter invites loitering,
just across from the base of a soaring
statue to *The Spirit of Industry.*
In the last quadrant there's nothing.
Unless you see a small contingent,
York Action for Peace,
determinedly, slowly circling

like animals pushing a stone.
Their signs and leaflets reaching out
to those to whom they are invisible.

Selected Poems

from *Rival Heavens* (1993)

Poem

Remembered backwards
like a dream,
from the breakup
to the first kiss,
a block of time
distinct
as the course
of an illness,
or the tenancy
of a house,
still recalled:
where the sofa was,
the window with no shade,
the hall that got no light,
details made vivid
by the invisible life within,
ghosts that fill their shapes
like breaths that form
a balloon . . . back
into that pre-everything
rootless time before we understood the lyrics
we were drawn to sing.

The Automobile That Hank Williams Rides In

New Year's Day, 1953

Confetti is scattered like seeds
on the sidewalks in front of bars,
Christmas trees roll in the gutter.
Out past the numbered houses,
along the main highway, the shadow
of a car bends around telephone poles
and guard rails, and flattens
on the long stretches of cinders
on the side of the road: It falls
below the bridge and races across
the gray water, leaping up again
on the bank. There is a wall of sundown
on the road. The light hitting the windows
of an elementary school on a hill
sets fire to the cut paper stars
and candles taped to the glass.
The shadow folds on the curb
of another town. The names
of the streets begin to rhyme.

Poem of the Dump Sticker Salesman

In a corner of the shack overnight
a spider has caught a wasp in its web
and has begun devouring it.
What becomes of the poison?
This morning townspeople come and go
buying their dump permits,
and in between I read your second book,
not rushed, but not as rich
as the first: Lists of plants
and flowers, and anonymous winds
have replaced people and their breath.
An easy voice has taken over
and left the hard things unsaid.
Later on, when it gets really quiet
I work on my own book, finished
many times, my second, third,
all unpublished, careful to put
them away when a customer comes,
then picking up again where I
left off, mid-poem, mid-career,
in a booth in a parking lot
selling dump stickers, surrounded
by the August traffic,
I keep going,
looking for the heart,
mindful of the poison.

Early Days

Early days,
still vivid,
rich in detail,
like so many books
you find, already
underlined, and with
scribbling in the margins
in the beginning,
then trailing off
to nothing, as if
left unfinished,
or finished without
comment: things like
a corner in November
where you stood deciding
which way, while
the debris of the city
swirled in the street
outside the spotlit window
of a department store,
and the woven whirlpool
of the cornucopia spilled
its plastic fruit
and candy corn
at the feet
of the mannequins.

And standing there,
willingly lost,

a future ghost
on streets that will
never be that new
or strange again,
not even when barely
recognized beneath
the snow's cold life mask,
or seen too closely
through a drug's
heartless lens.

O for a glimpse
of the knowledge
that is years off!
that must be forming
even now, under
the litter of empty days,
the way, back then,
a molten slat of light
was forged beneath
the dead weight
of a locked door:
the crack of *déjà vu,*
through which the past
and future slipped.

Because maybe now
the future is colder
and at the ends

of myself
there is nothing,
I forget the loneliness
and hunger of that time
spent searching
for the body
that fit mine
like the other half
of a treasure map,
and remember only
a day in late November
when the city welcomed me,
letting go a leaflet
behind the bandshell
in Union Square,
and wandering away,
down windy sidestreets
where newspaper rays glided
over the broken hulls
of packing crates
and busted pallets,
and Styrofoam dunnage
spilled on the curb
like worthless money.

Lost Friends

Friends end
and in your arms
and hands you feel
like you are
pulling a line
no longer attached
to anything
when their names come up
in conversation
or appear suddenly
at the bottom
of a drawer
leaving you
to examine
their lives in a tear,
magnified
like a drop
of pond water,
as it rolls across
the old envelope
in your hand,
the ink flowing again
after years
frozen in a name,
thawed
by the nostalgia
of a postmark,
the sun
of that time and place

now just another star
in an unfinished constellation.

The Anniversary

This must be the anniversary
of that day we drove
up on the mountains
and walked around
the empty buildings
of the church camp
where you spent a summer;
you wanted me to see
the carvings in the beams
done by refugees
after the war
but the doors were locked
and the windows boarded.
I don't remember what else
we talked about or thought.
It's like a scene in a foreign movie
when no one's speaking,
where there aren't any subtitles,
and the silence is in another language.
I only remember clearly how seeds
of the unmowed grass stuck
to the cuffs of my pants.
Why should I remember that?
Every day, however unimportant,
has and is an anniversary,
and though it was sunny
and warm then, and is cold
and raining hard now, today
must be the anniversary of that day

because, far from there,
driving alone, I thought of it,
and you, and the old thing.

The Lost

The wind blows across the lake
and through the trees
and shakes the hardwood branches
where each leaf hangs forlorn
as a lost glove on a bulletin board,
awaiting gravity's cold call, to jump,
back to earth, to mere existence,
after living in the air;
and all around the pines
stand soldier green.

The chains lie across the road,
the trails are open, but hardly
anyone comes in the park.
The only visitors this time
of year, in the middle of a weekday
afternoon, lonely souls who sit
in their cars in the empty lot
as big as the lake, or drive around
like they were looking for
a parking space, or a vacant table
through the trees; the same ones
you see on country roads, going slow as tractors,
as if they were lost,
which they are,
though they probably
know the route by heart.

I know where they are lost.
How in an empty room
the bowed head locks
and the eyes see through
the hands' bone fence,
and through the knees and legs
and floor, to a hidden spring
that is the source of tears;
and why they walk these paths
around dry fountains, the closed
concession stand and leaf-filled
barbecues, always staring down
like children who don't know the answer,
eyes averted from the certain chevrons
in the sky, drawn to the water's minutiae,
hypnotized by their survival play,
the salamander lifting the manhole
cover of a stone, the lives
below the acid roofs of leaves.

From the bridge above the dam
they see on one side the reluctance
of everything to go, even dead things,
and on the other how they do;
the snake bent double like a belt
hangs on a root, a branch
with the bark floated off,
smooth and hairless as a wrist,
clings with one finger of a twig.

They come to bathe their eyes
like icy pebbles on the bottom,
drown the loop of questions
in roaring falls, and,
with no place left to go,
retrace the only footsteps
on the beach, stopping
like an afterthought
to try to skip a stone
across the choppy surface,
then back again, against
the traffic, to the city,
home, the office
they called earlier to say
I can't come in today,
with whatever decision
they reached or postponed.

Driving to Maine

What did I think about
all that time
I was a child,
towering
over men at war,
hiding behind
a tree, backstage
memorizing lines?
Today, stalled
in layers of traffic:
planes overhead
raising or lowering
their landing gear,
and trains below
the expressway,
leaving the city,
pulling out of tunnels
in Charlestown, rock
flaking into shingle,
weeds along the bed
growing lush and spare
like laurel and rhododendron.
Rain since we left the Cape,
oblique, lonely angles
off of bridges down
into the streets
of dying downtowns,
silently through
a plate glass window,

into a mirror
in a beauty parlor,
or with the wind,
playing at the back
of a canvas newsstand
on the corner.
It was something like this,
being stuck in traffic,
without music, sitting
thinking nothing, that I did
for hours as a child.

If we could see
into our lives
through a window
like that, or with
the roofs lifted off
the mazes of early homes:
rooms and passageways
in apartments and schools;
floor plans we hammered
nails into, returned to abstraction,
to be the subjects
of dreams,
would we find
we passed or failed,
or the experiments
are just repeated
on a larger scale

for less and less reward,
a study of the effects
of time and entropy?
At Portland the exits
are impassable, the road
is a river. Hidden
from the narrow bridge
lightning pesters the walls
of the reactor core
of the nuclear plant
at Wiscasset.
When the storm is over
it is suddenly a dying day,
the sun devaluing from gold
and silver to copper
and clay; the trees
an evolutionary leap
since we saw them on the Cape.
Tonight I feel the fragileness
of something great,
like Earth's axis,
which tipped a few degrees
could scorch the planet
or freeze it lifeless;
and the giant elms at Bath,
succumbing to a fungus;
or the mind's daily
balancing over an abyss
it sees and shields from us,

knowing we falter when we try
to walk a tightrope,
even one drawn in chalk
across the dull macadam.

Passing floating granite
institutions, converted
mansions, set back
from the road,
the signs illegible
in heavy fog, private
and state run schools,
the high tension lawn
of an asylum. For many
the pain has been steady
since waking, in others
it is building to a scream,
much as laughter builds
in someone else
to overflowing.
Through the fog
like carving,
lettering a stone,
for whom?
Someone dying
no one knows?
Those inside
without a name?
All those lives

in the prison we pass
at Thomaston,
like a meteor shower
behind the clouds.

For Ellery

When my son asked
"We aren't in someone's hand are we?"
I said I didn't think so
and kept on walking,
feeling suddenly unprepared,
especially out-of-doors,
where the autumn sky
was the blue of deep space
and tilted with each step.
I didn't ask where he got the idea
but imagined him at the edge
of a group of children
listening to a retelling
of a Sunday school lesson,
or catching the refrain
of that old spiritual,
and remembering to ask me later,
at this moment, when I fail
to give an answer I am happy with,
but he seems satisfied
and moves on cheerfully
to another unrelated question
as if they're stored and stacked
all day for this occasion.

Yet the picture lingers:
us walking back together
from the post office,
by the abandoned garden

with the sun going down
behind the trees
at the marsh's edge,
all in the palm of a giant hand,
a medieval world view,
drawn from our collective childhood
before we knew the mechanics
of the universe, when
puffed cheeks blew sailing boats
across the woodcut seas,
or stripped the leaves
from branches while
a benevolent sun watched over
the gardener's shoulder.

That scene, untroubled,
comforting, a reminder
of the innocence beside me,
is laid across the present
like a transparency
so nothing matches
or lines up, except
the horizon which separates
the earth, now full of shadows,
from the lights
of rival heavens.

Childhood

It keeps getting darker
back there.
They are playing catch
with a luminous ball,
shooting baskets by sound.
The edges of the playground
close in
until it is
just the size of this room
grown suddenly cold
and quiet enough
to overhear them
walking home, their plans,
future secrets,
buried in silence
at the corner
where they part.

Youth

"Life is a burning up of questions."

– Antonin Artaud

To see it fade:
hill give way
to hill, tree
replace tree
on the highway's
endless loop,
where scenery
repeats itself
as if standing still
behind snow fences,
or seen through
the spokes of wheels
that slow to clock faces
as it darkens,
their hands moved forward
to an hour when
objects stand out
on the horizon,
stark and strange,
characters
in a foreign alphabet,
the language of use alone:
conveyor, corncrib,
tower, crane,
and so on, until
they're illegible
in the dark.

The city glows
behind a ridge
like a hidden airstrip.
Exits flurry and die out.
The single headlights
of derelict cars
come toward me
around a mountain of slag
like miners' lamps.
The sparse traffic
the dots and dashes
of a code spaced
too far apart
to make sense.

I reach for the coins
on the dashboard,
my hand green-veined
and blotched
in the anemic light
of the toll plaza,
and recall
those days when you
would lean over
with the change,
and we'd drive off,
rolling the window
back up to a crack
that let the smoke out

and the night air in:
and those long afternoons
the sun hung in a corner
of the white sky
like an erasure
on smudged paper,
and distant lightning
registered like a loose wire
jiggling in the radio,
the lights and wipers
of the oncoming traffic
already on,
then the rain,
steady and hard,
the sound coming
from all sides,
the glass alternately
blurred and clear,
like eyes fighting tears,
the other wiper
trying to lift
like a broken wing.

Where is all that sky
we traveled into?
Became breath.
And all those horizons
we crossed
like tar-filled

cracks
in the highway?
They become veins of ink
burning in a letter,
lines on a map
we can never go back to,
the roads lost
in the spring rain.

Reunion

Rain against the glass
like a handful of pebbles
tossed up from the street
where no one waits
beneath the swaying lamppost.
No old friend
steps from the dark
to rescue one tilting
with the solid objects
of the world, vulnerable,
if only for a moment,
to the patient voices
that prey on those
who lose their way,
whispering their truths
about this world
as viewed from another.
On the table, bound
in imitation leather,
the blue and gold
school colors, the roster
of the class of sixty-three,
a list of uninvited guests
with me tonight, replete
with blanks for those who
vanished into the great
American space, and left
no forwarding address;
and asterisks, the mechanical

stars shine in front of
those who fell before
mostly man-made death:
cars, drugs, and war.
Here a name you sought
for years, sometimes
almost absently, paging
the directory in distant cities,
and others unthought of
till this moment, equals
now in silhouette, the print
emboldened by the flashing
of the storm that races
up the coast. Each name
an unopened door,
the friend who moved away,
got sick, or changed:
the knob comes off
in your hand
like the short piece
of a wishbone,
and you wonder why
it broke where it did,
what forgotten lessons
must apply, and, what
no one can explain,
how such small things
can change the course
of a life: a busy signal,

letters crossing in the mail,
signal the end of love;
the time spent
waiting in a car
for a song to end
can save you
from a fiery fate
outside the door.
The water runs partway
down the window, pauses,
Then decides, or is
mysteriously guided
through its next
invisible maze, and
starts again at the top
like floaters in the eye
seen close up when staring
into the distance.
Exact details and data
do not always lead
to predictability
of the whole;
speeded up,
the process runs
to randomness,
at first trembling,
then buckling the bridge
into chaos, while
the far shore stands

mute and breathless
as the other side
of the door
you're banging on.
There are times
the lost life seems better,
to have run off the road,
been cut free, wondered at,
to be remembered differently,
in some way perfect,
while the rest grow old
and slow, to have been
through it all quickly,
and never have to see
the senses clog and fail,
the mind seize up
and harden like stone,
better to have lain down
in the broken glass
and shadows of the flashing
highway, felt the blood
rush to your side,
your life leap out.
Tonight in a hall in Pennsylvania,
no doubt too large,
and that never gets warm,
they're doing new steps
to old songs, and reminiscing
unreliably as any witnesses

and veterans of the same events,
matching faces and bodies
with name tags, so far removed
from when they saw each other
every day: passing papers
in homeroom, lagging
in corridors, asleep
in study hall, always
waiting for a bell.
Hundreds of miles away
I stare into the reflection
of this room outside
the window,
while the rain
pours through like light,
now cold and silent
as that fall, when
leaving hours of interrogation
where no notes were kept,
Oswald turned and saw,
between the shoulders
of the guards, his bruised
face at the barred window,
like another prisoner's,
wishing him luck.

Elegy

How many others
struggling today,
as the snow changes
to rain on the highway,
feel the walls
tear like cardboard,
as they walk out
to the road,
like walking out of a box,
kicking,
the sides flapping
and falling away?
Or make a wish
and blow the pilots out.

The stars of suicide
must have filled your room
with enormous light
for a moment,
I am not surprised;
sometimes
even a child's boat,
with paper sails,
catches that light,
out of reach,
in the middle of the lake,
tipping
in a real storm.

Even those little streams,
hardly noticeable bridge,
some concrete railing
along a road,
all nameless,
together make a river
several miles wide
and deep,
we may not
keep crossing
safely forever.

The lights in windows
and on porches
up and down the block
and the streetlights overhead
form a constellation
which rules tonight.
The lawn turns from green
to white, to the non-color
of freezing rain
lying on the grass
like the pebbled glass
of a door,
to a green room,
where the rain warms,
and a shadow
is coming to answer.

The Key

Finding an old key in the drawer,
I try to remember what it's for,
an old apartment, a car
on a hill somewhere
with weeds growing out of its motor.
I've forgotten.
I should throw it out
but won't, even though it couldn't
fall into the wrong hands anymore.
The locks are all broken or changed.
It probably opens a door in a wall
of doors around a building site
or lying in a stack on a wrecker's lot.
Yet it shines. Dull and unpretty,
it shines into a blind spot in the eye
where nothing is certain:
I may have forgotten someplace.
We may have to go back.
Tunnel through the years.
I will need this key.

from *Ladder of Hours* (2005)

On This Side

On this side
there are forests,
white in winter,
that turn in spring
a perishing green,
water that circles;
on its cloud-rain-sea cycle
tears are a step.
So are the lakes
that remember and forget
the sky all day.
There is the slow speed
of atoms in wood and steel,
and their racing in steam and breath.
On this side
we have bodies,
weightless at times,
at times stone.
On this side . . .
I could go on.
I could name everything.
But the names would soon
sound absurd, each like
the only word we know
in a foreign language,
and over there
nothing would hear anyway,
nothing sees.
On that side

it is darker than blindness,
and the silence is louder
than that which wakes us
suddenly, fallen asleep
to music or noise.

The Impossible Bouquet

Late at night
they appear together,
the friends of different eras
who never knew each other,
only you, but tonight
because a wall's collapsed,
from age perhaps, or simply
tiredness, they can have
a conversation, or appear
for once in the same picture,
like one of those 17th century
floral paintings the artists
worked on for months, incorporating
flowers from each season as
they blossomed, and allotting space
for those not yet in bloom,
creating in the end
an impossible bouquet.

What is it they are talking about,
so animated, yet still
under their breath, half heard
and only guessed, but from
a corner of the eye they seem
to be smiling, laughing,
each in his famous way.

The Somnambulist Blue

The somnambulist blue, narcotic sky
of early evening, when over the roofs
and wires and branches appear . . .
like something obvious suddenly remembered,
or seen, as in a picture that can be
looked at two ways, a puzzle drawing
from *The Children's Page,* whose gardens
and woods, spaces in thickets and trees,
endlessly hide faces; mouths formed
by a vine, eyes and hair made of leaves
and sky; so now, suddenly seen as always
there . . . appear, in the beginning of the night
above me, the stars, beautiful as questions:
Where is your hand? Are you asleep?

Night's Silence

1.

Night's silence
a space left blank
for answers. I fail
and have to read
myself to sleep,
and failing that . . . ?
The door is locked
on being awake
and alive. I think
of those who forced
the lock, how a thought
destroyed them, an image
or particular scene
that never went away
or lost its power.
And others I still share
this room with, in dawn,
or dark like this.

Scattered across time zones
in cities where we lived,
under skies the old white
of lead paint, or below
the brilliant violet midnight
in the country, are the calm
or agitated faces
of friends asleep,
at different angles

and stages, from night's
first dreams which skim
the surface of the day
for names and themes,
to other, deeper rooted ones
that end with light.

Each state fed blood
from the state before,
and sharing a light source,
dims and brightens
as we breathe,
and is accompanied by music,
though unheard, notes
struck by sleepers' hands
moving at their sides.

2.

Distance dwarfs mementos:
A scarf becomes a rag
in another city,
and the city is turned over
in a glove compartment
in a junkyard. Will I
ever see this town
as a dot on a map
and say *I lived there?*
It happened twice already.

Was it a blessing or a curse
when deep inland the plow
turned up a seashell?
Incongruous as that bottle
of Walden water saved
from a prep school pilgrimage,
that stood unopened,
undisturbed, brushed
by the hashish winds
and manic howls,
on the sill
of the phony window
between the rooms
in your apartment
on Second Avenue.
Where is it now?
Was it finally poured
into the New York City sewers,
or is it still in your bag, tossed
as you are tossed?

Between us
we probably have
more beginnings
than all the dead ends
of evolution,
the pigs with wings,
stones that spoke,
and walking flowers.

Once we saw
a starting sky
at the end of the street,
upright, gray,
a frozen stick of gum
between the buildings,
a tombstone of air
above the Hudson.

Remember Cuban bread
on the table
of the Pennsylvania farmhouse?
Outside the steamed-up windows
freezing rain,
at intervals
perhaps musical,
if heard on that scale,
instead of the hiss
of expensive gas
heating unheatable rooms,
and records repeating
endlessly as wine
fills coffee cups,
and from a corner
by the furnace,
comes, like signals
from another planet,
the sound of a typewriter
finding its first words.

3.

I am crossing years tonight
to light an answer.
What was then a handful
of cold water
dribbling back
through the fleshy cracks
of the fingers
into a pool,
is nothing now,
a cloud, many tears,
part of an ocean: memory.
And the illusory green
of the trees
and the familiar mud
and silver of the river
at Long Level, the sky
in litmus puddles
along the road—
the taste of wine
from an uprooted vineyard.

Self-Portrait in Pigshit

"All writing is pigshit." – Antonin Artaud

I did not think—
you could not think
in that space,
crouched on those flyblown boards
laid across the tops of the pens,
nails and hammer next to you,
balancing on the beam—
about that line
I'd laughed at years before.
It was so near,
and writing so far away,
as I looked down at the pigs
no longer curious enough
to look back, thank god,
with their human eyes
from the planned pitch
of the concrete floor.

That fall, on those rainy days
we could not go
on the job,
we stayed around the farm
and worked on the *finishing house.*
The hogs already in,
we had to put up
plywood panels that
would open like windows
in summer for ventilation

and close tight in winter to form
a wall against the wind and snow.
We'd lift the panel into place
and tack it there
while we screwed the hinges
and latches on,
then pulled the nails,
but you had to be careful,
if a nail fell into the shit below
you'd have to climb down
and get it, otherwise a pig
could eat it and die.

At noon, stinking, though we'd
hosed our boots
and shed our coveralls,
we were still barely welcome
at the diner down the road
where we ate every day.
It took days, even weeks
after we were done to lose
the smell. A faint
trace always lingered,
enough to take you back
to the days under the roof
beating with rain, and above
the circling, complacent hogs.

The young man smiling,
standing with his crew
in the doorway of Nellie's Café
greeted by a chorus
of catcalls and ribbing,
does not exist anymore.
Those cells are buried in the air.

Yet around his visage
there's a glow
as if someone has been breathing
on his picture, trying to bring
it closer, make it clearer.

In Matera

In Matera,
where the darkness
rose from the sockets
of caves
under the city,
like a town
in Pennsylvania where
the coal fires burn
miles down,
year after year,
unquenchable,
I dream again
of you, so seldom
in all this time,
and not even you,
but a stranger
with news of you:
a confusing, messy tale,
a custody battle, lost jobs.
I couldn't follow it all,
and what I could conflicted
with what I knew,
but like all dreams
it had a logic
which overrules
contradictions, as when
I see my dead father now,
in whatever improbable place
and wake

believing it was real,
so through this
intermediary I felt you near,
as in another room
listening, and at one point,
in the semi-darkness,
thought it might be you,
in disguise, and wearing
glasses you haven't worn
since high school.
Still, I would have recognized
the voice, in that strange place,
enclosed like a porch
in some equatorial region,
shuttered against the heat
of the day. What were
you trying to say?
Waking, I tried
to find my way back,
there is a way,
almost by vibration,
but it was lost, and you
receded like a train
pulling out of a station,
though really it was me
who was leaving.
In the morning,
in a cold hotel,
my wife and son

next to me,
our beds in a row
like a ward,
we rose and went
down into the streets
stained with the dust
of mountains and caves,
to a church built
to the dead, whose
crowned and laureled
skulls were carved across
the door, and skeletons
danced on the lintel.
An old woman in black let us in.
Sometimes there is no message.
Just a presence,
saying "I am not lost."

Homecoming

We drove through the gates
into a maze of little roads,
with speed bumps now,
that circled a pavilion,
field house, and ran past
the playing fields and wound
their way up to the cluster
of wood and stone buildings
of the school you went to once.
The green was returning to
the trees and lawn, the lake
was still half-lidded with ice
and blind in the middle.
There was nobody around
except for a few cars in front
of the administration. It must
have been spring break.
We left without ever getting out
of the car. You were quiet
that night, the next day,
the way after heavy rain
that the earth cannot absorb,
the water lies in pools
in unexpected places for days
until it disappears.

The Hitchhiker

I don't want to tell him
how much the place he's headed
has changed, that he won't even
be able to afford a beer there.
He looks ahead, sideways,
the sunlight mars his face,
shows he cannot
answer life's blows.
He's just an opponent now.
He digs for words. They
fall off a shovel, the stones
are names. The junk
I had to move to let him in
is still strewn across the floor
of the back seat. But his
breath on the window is gone.
I let him out near the center,
an easy walk. I know
before long, his clothes,
the crowds, youth, something,
will humiliate him.
The headlights home
will make him flinch again.

Treasure Island

For my son

Beside me
on the couch,
finally quiet
after running all day;
his knees stick out
like a pair of bruised peaches.

The room is bright,
a box of light
floating in darkness.
Windows on three sides open
so it's almost out-of-doors.
The noise of the swamp
drifts in: peepers,
and unknown wings
flapping, shaking loose,
bugs bouncing off screens,
the corners murmuring.

Although he can read now,
he'd rather listen,
like getting a ride
and watching the trudging
miles go by.
What does he see
as I read the description
of the bluff above the cove

where the pirate ship
lay anchored?
A hill nearby
where Truro
curves around the bay?
And he's Jack Hawkins I'm sure,
but who's the Squire, the Doctor,
and Long John Silver?

Citronella circulates
its smell from childhood,
now mimicking hashish,
and the lighthouse
from a mile off
casts its weak strobe
over land, together conjuring
another treasure hunt,
begun before you've got
an idea what you're
looking for, only
what it is not.
Behind the laced sugar water
taste the metal of the spoon,
like blood, and hear again
the heroic music turning tinny,
as everything slows
like a film caught until
it burns in front of
the projector's naked bulb,

a light behind the eyes
that won't go out.

That time is kept alive
like a match cupped
against the wind, a candle
in a skull, flickering tonight
in uneven breaths,
as sleep,
the dark sub-text,
the undertow
in the story-teller's voice
pulls him under, and carries
him off to an island
overgrown with the vegetation
of dreams and peopled
by composites
from the day's dismemberment
by clock hands.

Then, subtly altered, its mass
magnetized, his head
is charged with dreams,
and leaning next to mine
generates their waking
counterpart: wishes,
but all in the negative:
may he avoid this,
be spared that,

not have to go through
something else . . . the list
cuts out a silhouette, faceless,
blind with bliss,
while I revisit another night,
an afternoon stretched into evening
in a dealer's pad on Eleventh Street,
across the table from Bobby Driscoll,
who, someone told me later,
"played the kid in *Treasure Island.*"

Even the small town paper
I was reading a few years later
carried the wire service obituary,
an overdose:
a clear proof of something
still unclear.
That night
when his connection came
he broke off talking
and tied his ascot
around his arm
and hunted for a vein,
then leaned back, eyes filled
with appreciation, overwhelmed
as soundless applause
spanned the living pain
separating the same person
years apart.

The dark is lined with fur,
fins, and feathers
rustling and fluttering,
their sudden silence
a trip wire across the lawn
leading to the swamp
where the tireless lighthouse
flashes its ambiguous message:
equal parts safety and danger,
and its strobe shows
the night at work:
its jumping eyes, and vines
of climbable shadows,
and interlocking circles
like magician's rings
spreading across the water
as rain brings music,
changing tempos, slowing, adding
a thousand strings
in all directions: so many
leaves struck, grasses bent,
and branches glazed.
He stirs at its cold scent;
a shiver runs through him,
then me. It's late
I mark our place.

Revolution in the Air

Reading how this party split
into two factions, one of which
survived into the '90s, the other
dissolved almost immediately
over disagreements as to whether
to concentrate on cadre-building
or developing alliances within
the working-class . . .
I had to keep one finger
in the back, in the glossary,
to keep track of who's who,
and remind myself these acronyms
had faces, marched on sunny days,
in rain and wind, argued
endlessly the course of events
that never came but flowed away
from them on a tide of breaths
propelled by heartbeats, little oars
that move us closer, through
narrowing passageways,
to the future's source.

February

The murder of Malcolm X
took place long ago
but now he's everywhere,
coming up from underground
the first thing you see,
books with his face on the cover
on a cloth spread out
on the sidewalk next to T-shirts
on which a splotch of colored ink
mixes with nothingness
to form his eyes, the edge
of the familiar jaw and brow.
He was in transition then,
the crowds that themselves
were thinking, rethinking,
knew it was important, even brave,
to come, the nadir of the winter,
dark hole of the week, Sunday
afternoon, the street all dirt
and wind, corrupted snow.
That is also when Horowitz
always played, Sunday
afternoon, at 4 P.M. . . .

He was dead by then,
on stage, among cables
and wires from microphones
and tape recorders,
freed from his age

in its swollen strings,
untuned, like a bead
curtain you push aside
to enter a room
denied to others.

Poem

I felt nothing
driving by your city,
no magnet tug
greater than any other,
just old water tanks,
oil reserves, malls
and miles of fast-food restaurants
and struggling storefronts
pulling for a different
reason; none of it
has any hold on me,
but looking down
those long streets
of little houses,
with trees grown up,
the driveways overflowing,
and the shining acres of cars
bowing down before
a single god, I didn't
hear one heartbeat
above the motor,
or words like music
caught in the hollows
of a swing set,
or any other place
the air stagnates:
a box with grass
and water, stars
punched in the top
so we can breathe.

Little Elegy

Even the stars wear out.
Their great engines fail.
The unapproachable roar
and heat subside
as wind blows across
the hole in the sky
with a noise like a boy
playing on an empty bottle.
It is an owl, or a train.
You hear it underground.
Where the worms live
that can be cut in half
and start over
again and again.
Their heart must be
in two places at once, like mine.

Working in Winter

We could fall.
The branches are slippery enough.
January in the top of a maple.
A tree-saw hanging from my belt.
Who are you?
What are you doing up there?
The sidewalk blows away.
It feels good. The air is crazy,
filling with snow. Cars maneuver
around the piles of branches
in the street. The cuts
smelling of fresh wood.
The snow and sawdust
falling together.

Some Nights,

between the car and door
in the dark
I look up to find
the great river
of the Milky Way,
and stand for minutes
growing cold
in the autumn air,
unable to move,
take my eyes away,
only to look back,
wishing the house
would vanish,
and I was alone, far from lights and roads
with *its* dark, *its* cold,
its change
from everything known,
which makes even
those reaching claw-like
backyard trees
seem welcoming,
and I think this must be
how innocents are drawn
into madness,
a whispering begins,
that could be anything, the wind,
but then turns definite,
becomes a voice that has
but one intended listener.

In a field years ago
I watched another river, dark,
without a name or end, flow overhead,
hundreds of thousands of birds,
the complete opposite, the negative
of that silent, lifeless stream of stars.

The cornfield is gone, so are the birds,
though their descendants may
still follow that same flyway,
perhaps some stars are also dead,
and only their light survives
like a memory a million years old.

Tired and cold, under
icy reminders of how insignificant,
how brief we are, I mouth
their message in words I see
disintegrate: I am alone;
I am almost nothing.
Yet these rivers meet in me.

Lullaby

The painful series
of operations that
culminate in death:
becoming forty, eighty,
neither one. Dying young
or old, awake or drugged,
or pleasantly unaware
in sleep as they say Auden
wanted to and did, with just
the slightest sensation,
like a sleeping baby
handed from one pair of arms
into another.

The Doorway,

seen a thousand times,
then changed suddenly,
the same steps followed
again and again
in the alchemist's experiment,
the same ingredients each time
except the time and its spirit,
leads to this room
where we stand by accident
and for a moment the dark lock
we live in is lighted
and we breathe the key.

At the Art Students League, 1965

1.

The evening classes over,
the students and instructors,
models and monitors, gone;
the building finally empty,
the staircase clear
which was crowded all day,
and in the studios the plaster
busts and crockery,
the cloths that drape
the pedestals wait to be
arranged a billionth time,
unexceptional except
they appear in drawings
and paintings on walls, in closets,
from here to Sacramento.
And around the room easels,
carefully placed like models,
hold their pose all night,
waiting to be changed.

In the cafeteria
on the floor below,
legs up, the chairs
like cartoon dead,
stacked on tables;
no din of trays or silver
disturbs the stillness.
Every table is empty, available,

where generations
fought their battles,
and salt and pepper shakers,
and catsup bottles, and
napkins just so, illustrated
points lost upstairs in paint.

Finally dark but for
the regulation lights above
the stairwell and exits,
and outside the "smoker,"
where we held critiques
and I first learned
the amazing range
of self-justification
and of the need to please:
I want the colors to be muddy.
Or *Do you think I should*
take the faces out?
Would it be better
greener, grayer, redder?
Acquiescing to the slightest doubt,
or most contradictory suggestions.
Our teacher told the story,
not apocryphal, but
coming true each day,
of a painter in the forties,
who made black, instead

of white, the basis of his palette,
adding a little to each color,
to unite and pull together
the disparate elements:
The black now showing through,
his paintings darken yearly.

I pictured them like
portraits in ancestral homes,
or hung too near a chimney:
flesh turning gray, sockets
deepening as eyes recede
beneath layers of soot
and smoke. Only these
paintings, which parody
inherent vice, darken
from within, and no amount
of cleaning will bring them back.

Now the darkest building
on the block, a hole
that sucks in light . . .
names and faces first,
the voices last . . .

2.

I no longer paint
but look at paintings

as if they were
extensions of that self,
relics of an unlived life.

Of the others I suppose
only the dullest were
unswayed by the continuous
music of the street, or
words from platforms that bent
each mind and heart
in new trajectories.

Whoever was not drawn
into the maelstrom,
where action vied
with contemplation,
sacrifice with self-indulgence,
has nothing now to say;
who never grasped
"the something more":
that art is just a hook
to draw us back
to a place
we've been
before there was art
but now cannot reach
without it.

Paperweight

Everywhere,
defeated beauty:
in old pines,
toothless
against the sky
brand new each day;
in rivulets
running in the grooves
of the stones,
eroding the banks
of their lettering,
till they belong
to no one again,
names called out
to no reply
over crackling P.A. systems,
disembodied sound
that floats until it's hoarse
and breaking up
like fireworks
crumbled
on the velvet sky.
In the longing
that loses its way . . .
A vein drags
these words to light,
like nets
set out to dry,
stretched across the rocks

for mending,
then forgotten,
the sea-smell
blowing off,
the hand-tied knots
undone, tons of cold
green water pushing up,
full of bubbles
like this glass
paperweight
on the yard-sale table.

When the Air Rushes In

When the air rushes in
where we have been
and our absence is everywhere;
when the sky full of insects and birds
fills up the space where we stood
and a hummingbird stalls in your heart
and a crown of bees circles my head;
and when the grass pushes back
the last trace of this weight
and our footsteps climb with the dew;
may these words remember us,
when our breaths have blown away
and our names have turned to stone.

On Breaking a Chain Letter

To Louise Glück

Let it end with me,
"this little prayer"
that has been around the world
nine times and has brought good luck
in the form of seven thousand dollars
to an American officer and sixty thousand
to Don Elliott, who lost it because
he broke the chain, and death
to Gen. Welsh in the Philippines
six days after he failed to send it on:
Let it end with me
so all my future disasters
can be explained.

Tightrope

One end is tied in my heart,
this voice that goes out
past my body, well past
my line of sight, places
I've never been,
arcades and alleys,
in fog and sun,
over dark fields turning light,
over water rushing,
into winter, into rooms. . . .
Where the other end is tied
I have no idea, I only feel it,
perhaps in another heart—
I walk toward it.

from *Cold Storage* (2016)

The Etymology of Halo

What you are working towards,
even in those hours spent
staring into the void
hoping to bring back strength
to hold down impulse
and raise the spirit
through a rain of blows,
comes not from heaven,
nor is that ring from
the finger of god, but is
instead a circle worn
on the threshing floor,
a path poor animals
made by constant turning.

A Strange Place

Sometimes you feel
a drop out of nowhere
on your skin
even on a clear day,
but because
it is just one
and gone instantly,
you don't think about it,
it doesn't stay
like déjà vu, that room
imposed on yours,
so when you enter one
you enter both.

Watchmen
who've fallen asleep
so often, so deep,
sometimes wake
not knowing where
or who they are.
That moment
a drop could fall.

Earth becomes more beautiful
as it gets older,
age doesn't matter to it,
it's already absurdly ancient,
but instead of appearing
stale and tired,

it feels fresh, new,
like the same words
shifting back and forth
between question
and answer.

And I can't tell you
if you ask,
whether this
child's collection:
pinecones, feathers, shells,
is about life or death.

New Year's Underground

This subway map
reminds me
of the colored stripes
on hospital floors
that guide us
to recovery
or dead ends
(I lift my glass
to the amber line)
or the spacious room
that overlooks
a beautiful parking lot
where the car roofs
are like tiles
you'll soon be walking on
in the same sunshine,
just a little older,
paler, having seen
the blizzard of empty beds,
too much aluminum,
so many shaky starts.

In this howling tunnel
they come into focus:
lemon, pink, lime,
the corner where a couple
stands aside to let you pass,
motioning you forward
while murmuring *red,*

red, waiting for
their strength to return.

The lines are like the nerves
and veins themselves
that are having trouble now,
that somehow got intertwined
or clogged, yet here they
cross without difficulty
or getting tangled up or lost,
regrouping at the intersection,
then heading off again
on separate missions,
sometimes shadowing
each other for awhile
until the lungs pull away
from the heart
with a jolt like a train.

Underground,
below the city streets,
stores, and high-rises,
the celebration leads
to sober reflection,
reassessments and the desire
to work to change,
but not today, where
we're sandwiched between
the past and what's not

yet arrived.
I'm lost
between the revelers
with one more stop,
and those who've
already had their cup
of sweetness on a tray.

If I Could Throw My Voice

like a ventriloquist,
I would make it speak
through the lamp

beside your bed,
when moonlight
chisels features

on the marble pillow
with its chiaroscuro
deepening the edges,

leaving high cheekbones
and flat planes
sunken and breathing solemnly

while the heart
roars like a furnace
fed the memories of a lifetime.

And I would have it say
I am sorry for the place you're in,
the strings that pull you

out of bed each morning,
wake you in someone else's arms,
and I would tell you that it's me

who hovers near
when in between
the carefully designated minutes

of your day a blank appears
like the unfinished pre-dawn sky
that hasn't decided

if it's white or gray or blue,
and for a few moments
cradling your coffee you

think of nothing, miss nothing,
look forward to nothing,
and I would

cut the strings right there
and let you stay,
attended by a ghost

that envelops
and protects you like
the fog off the bay

which softens and erases
edges, corners, faces,
which don't register, words

that don’t belong,
including these from
who knows where.

Rain

Rain is the great transporter,
even before it arrives
its perfume slips under the door
like a letter, an invitation to rise
as earthbound drops
descend like weights
backstage raising the scenery
and lifting us out of easy chairs
and easy lives,
to where it never rains,
is always parched, a room
cut off and boarded up,
and where a single drop
on those lips
could bring you back.

A Handful of Gravel

The day's magic:
fairy dust
or just
the pink
eraser crumbs
that make a name,
an address,
vanish.

The block
you stumbled on:
windows & doors
reflecting
back and forth
across the traffic,
infinity's
fake façade.

Run your fingers along
the goose-bumped flesh
of stairwell walls,
the hard sea-green enamel,
trailing dirt and grime
from stoop
to rooftop clothesline:
skirts and sheets
pollinated with soot.

When you arrive
at the last memory
will it be shiny,
bright, having been
hidden all this time,
or dark, confused,
as a tarnished mirror
no one's looked into
for years?

A handful of gravel mid-air,
tossed at the darkened window,
a constellation
real as those
that control our destiny.

In a year
this will be woven
into the fabric
of what's over.
And their failure,
falling back,
like the beginning
of an avalanche,
is the failure of all
returning to a path.

To One Who Owes Me Money

To finally locate you
after all these years
and then—
it's in a dream!:
You're near the end
in a hospital
in a small New England city,
what monstrous snake
of a road led you here,
where you sit on the bed
making calls as you did,
to the rich and famous,
trying to raise money
for your wife's pathetic project,
and by extension, us, laboring
within earshot of your makeshift
desk. They were never home
to you, always at lunch
or in a meeting. I don't think
I ever heard you get through
to anyone. It was forty years ago.
The money you owe me would
be a fortune now. I could use it.
But I needed it then, as I have
almost every year since.
You used it to run away
with your wife and daughter
to England, and then
with your daughter

away from your wife
back to America.
You were a fool under her spell,
and when the spell was broken. . .
well, we all fear the day
the endearing, idiosyncratic traits
turn to irritants and hideous faults,
the way a clown's face goes
to scary after funny. We loaned
you strength on those filthy floors
overlooking Second Avenue,
tearing down walls, pulling
through the lathing old horse hair
from the century before,
as outside it went from winter
to spring and early summer,
and all we took away were
a few indelible songs
from the radio, news
that kept getting shriller,
and a sense that what happened here
would always be tested, weighed
against another life that spoke
in anger and in silence,
and whose outstretched claw
you passed each day in the street.
Painting, sheet-rocking, we gave
up months of life's best season: youth.
Now you've returned the only way

you could to pay your debt, and left
this poem. We'll call it even.

From the Pilgrim Monument

For Roger Skillings

The climb is breathtaking,
the view roughly medieval:
On one side, the town's
boat-filled harbor
and traffic-clogged streets;
on the other, graveyards,
mute and still, stretching to the edge
of the moon-like dunes,
forever changing, shifting,
being taken away (the tallest one
already halved since we arrived here
thirty years ago) and nothing
added or put back except
beach grass planted to slow
the process, and a little dust,
ashes of friends who loved it here,
and wanted to stay or go
wherever it is going.

Fragment

You could be rowing across a parking lot
full of strangers who don't see you,
or drifting silently through the thick walls
of an institution, when you reach that shore.

And whatever you have on, even
a plain hospital gown, that will be your robe
for the ceremony that takes place in your
last breath, held before you like a lantern.

Fall of the Magician

"Water is slate, far down." – Weldon Kees

One great trick—
you can make your life disappear.
There's no one to thank for this.
No one thinks of it
except you, or if
they're suddenly removed
from their element
and going uphill slowly
around traffic cones
(they're working
on the Sagamore Bridge again),
and the water down there,
kept from us, is still
as the roof of another world.

Reminder

They put a clock
beside you
in your bed,
a reminder
of your mother‘s
heartbeat. The loud
ticking was supposed
to help you sleep
not keep you awake,
but how could that
cold metal sound like
her soft breath
or whisper? Now
it’s the back-beat
that follows you
into the street
where it drowns
arguing horns,
the noise of crowds,
but not the steps
on sidewalks
late at night
that prove the world
is hollow.

This Candle

In the end
there is always
a little change
left in the pockets,
a few suns and moons
you couldn't spend.

Nearby
the cloud
of a would-be breath
doesn't move,
reprieved
but useless.

This candle
will change all that,
use the last bit
of air for light,
and heat the hand
that shields the eyes
and face when it gets
too close or bright.

No one speak.
The dark
will say a few words
about our friend,
leave it at that.

For Mary Oliver, Leaving Provincetown

Goodbye, Mary.
That's hard to say.
My mother's name was Mary.
It is also hard to see
part of your life
drift away, if only
symbolically.
You are the last
of the boundary stones
I found here.
Remember the others'
high-pitched rhetoric,
their drunkenness, sulking
and raving, storming out.
Plenty of scenes. Now
it is just you, going quietly
someplace where you'll no doubt
find sister and cousin birds,
louder, fatter, southern versions
of the same species you startled here
on your morning walks.

Therefore I expect
to learn soon
that you've discovered
in the new beauty
of that place,
something moving
just below the surface,

half fin, half claw,
which spoke to you
in a string of bubbles
and you answered in a voice
thin and rough as beach grass
anchoring a dune.

Against Closure

Memory weakens the heart,
reliving all those scenes,
half-running up the hill,
flesh visible between
shoulders of the rescue workers,
and a cloud, far off, delivering rain
to a corner of the city. Now
would be the perfect time
to weigh those things,
in a pressure-free environment,
but with the scales missing,
or broken, chain lying
in the trays,
everything weighs the same—
nothing. So we can't
measure what we've done,
and the story, like a movie
seen a hundred times,
should lose its power,
yet still you look away,
let a shudder run through
worn flesh and bone.

The Road

You started following a light,
hearing a call from a place
far beyond your narrow bed.
And once in a while you saw
or heard it again in the street
hurrying along with envoys
from the other world,
“hastily-put-up men,”
who were actors in a play
you wandered into.
They knew their lines,
you had to improvise yours.
You did. For years
in ever smaller quarters,
cramped by desire,
weighed down by
the iron gall of letters.

Then you found equilibrium
in a storm, a torrent,
blizzard where you could not see
the road ahead or behind,
and you moved in fear
and would have stopped
had not the storm
stopped before you. Now
whatever you meant,
whatever made you
follow in the first place

is gone. Your work is done.
Nothing's left but the plain gray
sky that goes on forever
and makes you long
to start again.

Keith Althaus is the author of three poetry collections, *Rival Heavens, Ladder of Hours,* and *Cold Storage,* which won the 2016 Off the Grid Poetry Prize. He has also received a Pushcart Prize and grants from the National Endowment for the Arts and the Massachusetts Foundation of the Arts. His work has appeared in *The New Yorker, Harper's, Poetry,* and *Ploughshares,* among others. In 1969, he was one of the first Writing Fellows at the Fine Arts Work Center in Provincetown, Massachusetts. He lives on Cape Cod with his wife, the artist Susan Baker.